GLENDA'S LONG SWIM

Glenda's Long Swim

Richard A. Boning

Illustrated by

Harry Schaare

The Incredible Series

Barnell Loft, Ltd. Baldwin, New York

To

Jeanne Chall

Glenda and Robert Lennon had anchored their new motorboat in the Gulf of Mexico—over four miles offshore. The young couple from Eustis, Florida, were fishing in the area for the first time. The sea was calm and they were enjoying the warm Florida sun. Nothing about the water suggested danger.

Robert cast his line, as Spunky, their pet poodle, sniffed at the bait can. Then, at 2 PM, Glenda decided to try some spearfishing. She put on rubber flippers, a snorkel, and a glass face mask. Grasping a spear gun, she jumped into the water and swam about twenty-five yards beyond the boat. Unknown to Robert and Glenda, however, tides and ten-knot winds from the east were building up an unusually strong outgoing current.

Glenda playfully chased fish through the crystal-clear water for a quarter of an hour. Then she heard Robert call, "You're drifting! Swim back!" She was surprised to find herself nearly forty yards from the boat.

Glenda struggled, but to her amazement, she made no headway. She was a fair swimmer, but Robert was an expert and had won many events in state and national contests. He swiftly dived in and was soon beside her.

He took the spear gun from Glenda, and they began swimming toward the anchored boat, but it seemed to be growing smaller and smaller in the distance. Despite their efforts, they were being pulled out to sea by a current of eight knots—a current stronger than Robert had ever felt before.

"Look!" cried Glenda. Spunky had followed Robert off the boat, and now the dog was being swept past them toward the open sea. "Help her," Glenda pleaded. Robert swam after the frightened Spunky, and in moments he had her by the collar. Again he found himself struggling against the current. Slowly he towed the dog toward Glenda.

As Glenda tucked the poodle into her arms, Robert grappled with their problem. The outgoing current had just begun and would continue for hours. Rescuing the tiny dog had taken much of his strength. If he had to pull his wife all the way to the boat, he knew he could never reach it.

He looked at her tenderly. She was worried, yet her eyes expressed confidence in him. Somehow he must make it to the boat alone, and then he could motor back for Glenda. In the meantime, she must stay afloat.

The boat, now 200 yards distant, looked less than an inch high. Soon it would disappear. Robert was not at all sure he could reach it. Nor was he sure that Glenda could survive the savage current by herself.

Forcing himself to speak calmly, he told her he must go after the boat. Then he would come back and get her. While he was gone, she must tread water. "Don't use up any more energy than necessary," he warned. "Just keep moving your legs as slowly as you can. When you have to, move your arms."

Glenda nodded. "The fins will help you stay afloat," Robert reassured her. "If you get tired, lie face down. You can breathe through the snorkel."

"What about Spunky?" she asked.

Robert glanced at the little dog. "If she begins to tire you, let her go," he said firmly. Then he told Glenda, "It will take some time, but I'll be back as soon as I can."

They looked at each other for a long moment. Glenda could not remember ever treading water longer than a few minutes. Yet there was no other way. "All right," she whispered, "I'll wait for you." Robert swam away. Although he was a champion swimmer, he had not trained for several years. He quickly found that he could make no progress against the current. Then he realized that he must keep the boat in sight, without exhausting himself. When the tide turned, he would try to reach it.

Robert knew that each swimming stroke uses a different set of muscles. From time to time he changed strokes, to rest some of his muscles for the long ordeal ahead. He tried stroke after stroke—the crawl, the backstroke—even the butterfly. All that afternoon he fought against the current. He swam as never before. The boat was still in sight, and soon the current would slacken. Then he would use his remaining strength to swim to the distant craft.

After what seemed an eternity, the current weakened, then stopped altogether. Robert began to make headway toward the boat, which he could now see only from the crests of waves. Suddenly, he became aware of a new problem. The sun was setting! If he did not reach the boat before darkness, he would have no chance of finding it. The thought of Glenda's growing peril drove him on.

Robert's breathing was labored. Each stroke became more painful. Where was the boat? Just before the sun disappeared, he glimpsed a flash of reflected sunlight from the craft. With a desperate burst of strength, he swam toward it. Finally the hull loomed before him in the twilight. Somehow he managed to struggle aboard.

He had been swimming for well over six hours. For a moment he lay on the deck, gasping for breath. Then, forcing himself to his feet, he started the engine and began a four-mile sweep of the darkening waters. There was no sign of Glenda. His spirit shaken, he clicked on his transmitter and called out the code word of distress, "Mayday! Mayday!" No one answered. Wasn't *anyone* listening? Again he tried. A voice boomed from the receiver. It was the captain of a shrimp boat. Robert quickly explained his plight.

"Stay where you are," said the captain of the shrimp boat. "We need your position to set a course." To his relief, Robert could hear the alarm being spread throughout the entire fleet of shrimp boats. Still he was worried. So much time had passed. Could they find Glenda? Was she still afloat?

Glenda *was* still afloat. It had been over six hours since she had watched Robert swim away! All that time, she had continued to move her legs just enough to stay afloat. She was able to breathe with the snorkel, even when water swept over her head.

Glenda continued to cling firmly to Spunky, but the poodle began to sense the growing danger and became panicky. She tried to climb on top of Glenda. "No, Spunky," Glenda pleaded. "Stay down." If she couldn't control the dog, they would both go under.

Glenda spoke softly to Spunky, trying to comfort her. For a while the dog seemed to be satisfied. Then Spunky began to bark frantically and claw at Glenda. The effort to control the dog became too much. Glenda knew that she could hold her no longer. Sadly, she let her pet slip from her arms. "Goodbye, Spunky," Glenda whispered. The small poodle was swiftly carried off by the current. Glenda forced herself to look away.

From the top of a wave, she could see that the boat was only a speck on the shoreless horizon. Robert was nowhere in sight. As the sun sank into the ocean, Glenda felt the powerful current pulling her still farther out into the Gulf. In a few minutes the sky grew purple. Then came hours of darkness.

To her dismay, Glenda felt the wind quicken. A bolt of lightning crackled above. In moments the storm struck. Sheets of rain lashed the whitecaps. Waves that had been only two feet high now surged over her head. Water splashed into her snorkel, and she gagged. The once-warm water grew cold. She was forced to move her arms and legs faster to stay afloat. They began to ache even more. With mounting dread she began to wonder if she could survive the storm. Finally, after what seemed hours, it ended and the ocean grew calm.

Before long, a glow of lights appeared on the horizon. Search craft! Her heart leaped with joy. Robert must have reached the boat. Soon she would be rescued. She would be safe and warm. But as time passed, she realized that the search boats were not getting any closer. They were much too close to shore.

From a distance came the faint drone of an engine. As it grew louder, she saw blinking lights approaching in the sky. A helicopter! The pilot dropped a parachute flare that turned the whole scene an eerie red. Now the helicopter was so close that she could read the numbers on its underside. She shouted and waved—but it faded into the distance, dropping other flares.

Then even the lights from the search boats began to wink out—one by one. The searchers were turning back to shore. They were giving up. She wanted to cry out, "Don't leave! I'm still alive!"—but she knew it would do no good.

A new fear gripped her. Maybe Robert had never reached the boat, and the searchers had been looking for both of them! Never had she felt so alone.

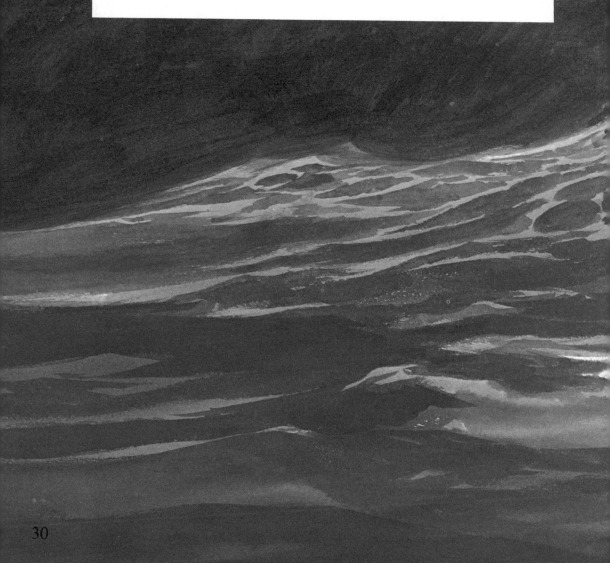

Suddenly, Glenda felt something brush against her leg. She froze with horror. Peering into the dark water, she expected to see the open jaws of a giant shark. Instead, she found herself surrounded by a school of tiny fish. They nibbled at her legs. Her flesh stung from the bites. Alarmed, she pulled away and kicked, and the fish disappeared.

She began to feel terribly cold. Briskly she rubbed her arms and legs. The warmth slowly returned, but the effort had taken more of her waning energy. Glenda began to feel drowsy. She rested her head in the water and dozed, breathing through her precious snorkel.

Later she awoke beneath a star-sprinkled sky. She thought of Robert and their two-year marriage and all the fun they had shared. It had been wonderful. Was this the way it was meant to end?

In time the sky changed from velvet black to pearl
gray. Soon the horizon was tinged with pink. With the
dawn would come the answer. "If there are any boats,
I'll see them," she said aloud. But when the sun rose
like a bright balloon, the vast ocean was empty. Only a
lone white pelican glided overhead. It was then that
Glenda began to accept the fact that she would soon die.

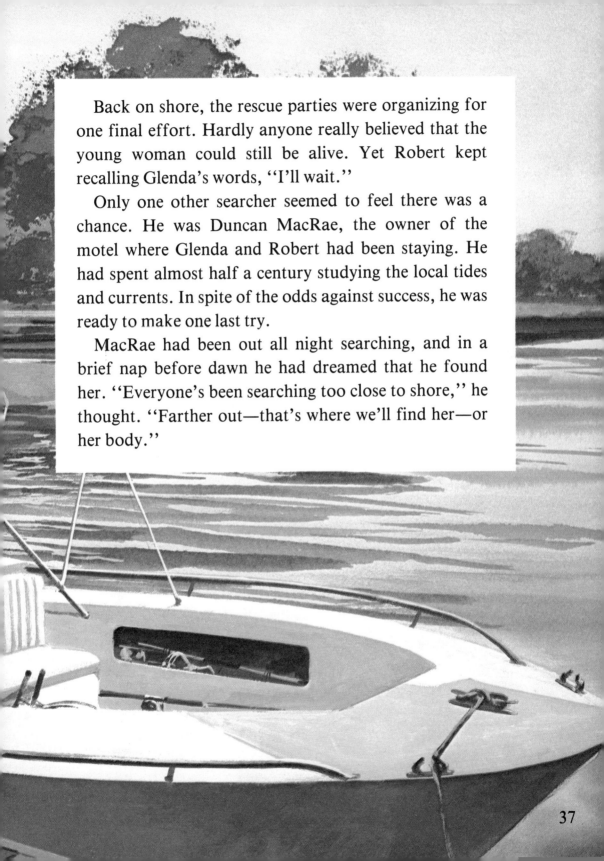

Back on shore, the rescue parties were organizing for one final effort. Hardly anyone really believed that the young woman could still be alive. Yet Robert kept recalling Glenda's words, "I'll wait."

Only one other searcher seemed to feel there was a chance. He was Duncan MacRae, the owner of the motel where Glenda and Robert had been staying. He had spent almost half a century studying the local tides and currents. In spite of the odds against success, he was ready to make one last try.

MacRae had been out all night searching, and in a brief nap before dawn he had dreamed that he found her. "Everyone's been searching too close to shore," he thought. "Farther out—that's where we'll find her—or her body."

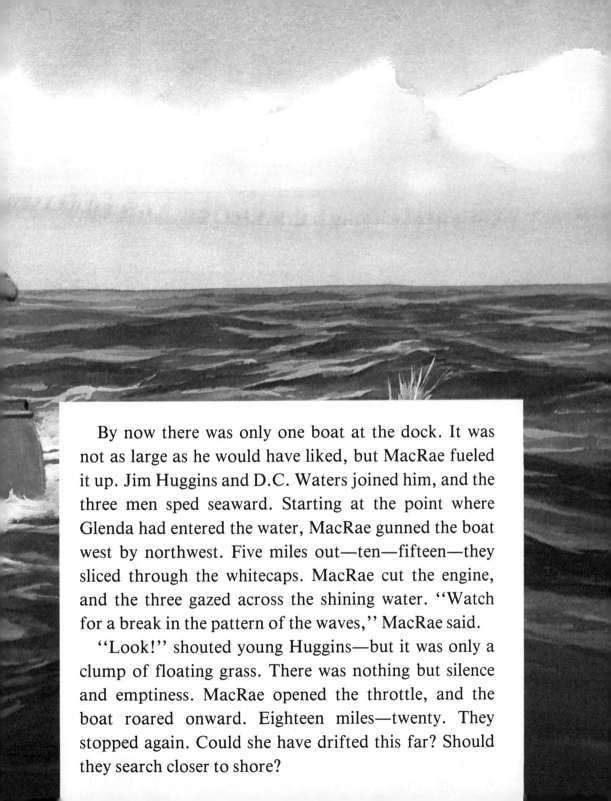

By now there was only one boat at the dock. It was not as large as he would have liked, but MacRae fueled it up. Jim Huggins and D.C. Waters joined him, and the three men sped seaward. Starting at the point where Glenda had entered the water, MacRae gunned the boat west by northwest. Five miles out—ten—fifteen—they sliced through the whitecaps. MacRae cut the engine, and the three gazed across the shining water. "Watch for a break in the pattern of the waves," MacRae said.

"Look!" shouted young Huggins—but it was only a clump of floating grass. There was nothing but silence and emptiness. MacRae opened the throttle, and the boat roared onward. Eighteen miles—twenty. They stopped again. Could she have drifted this far? Should they search closer to shore?

Suddenly MacRae saw the sun glint on something far out in the water. They raced toward it. To their joy they saw a tiny figure bobbing in the sea, waving feebly. Glenda!

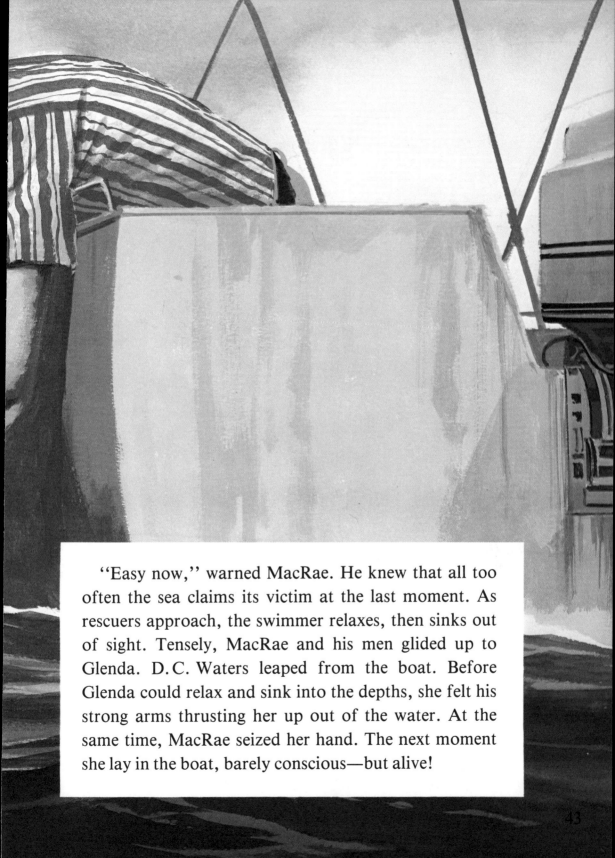

"Easy now," warned MacRae. He knew that all too often the sea claims its victim at the last moment. As rescuers approach, the swimmer relaxes, then sinks out of sight. Tensely, MacRae and his men glided up to Glenda. D.C. Waters leaped from the boat. Before Glenda could relax and sink into the depths, she felt his strong arms thrusting her up out of the water. At the same time, MacRae seized her hand. The next moment she lay in the boat, barely conscious—but alive!

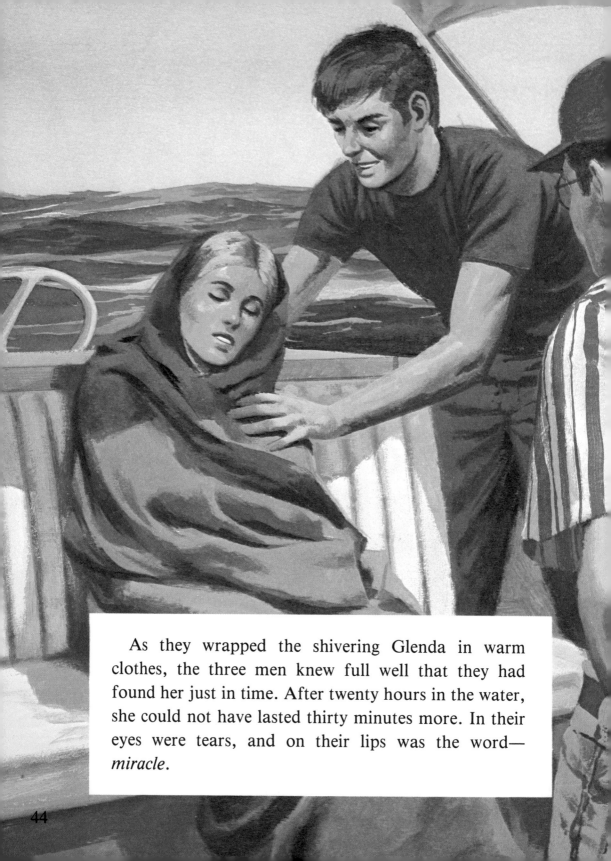

As they wrapped the shivering Glenda in warm clothes, the three men knew full well that they had found her just in time. After twenty hours in the water, she could not have lasted thirty minutes more. In their eyes were tears, and on their lips was the word— *miracle*.

Speeding shoreward, they met Robert's boat. When he saw Glenda, he leaped joyfully to her side. She looked up and smiled weakly. He felt a lump rise in his throat, and his eyes grew misty.

"I waited," Glenda whispered, "just as you said." He held her close as the boats headed homeward. The long, terrifying swim of Glenda Lennon was over.